TREASURE ISLAND

Scale 2 English Miles
Spyglasse Hill
Bulk of Treasure
Swamp
Stockade
Graves
Mizzenmast Hill
Skelton Island
Treasure Island
Aug. 1, 1750 J. F.
Given by above J. F. to Mr W. Bone
Mate of ye Walrus
Savannah this twenty July 1754
W. B.
Facsimile of Chart, latitude and longitude struck out by Jim Hawkins

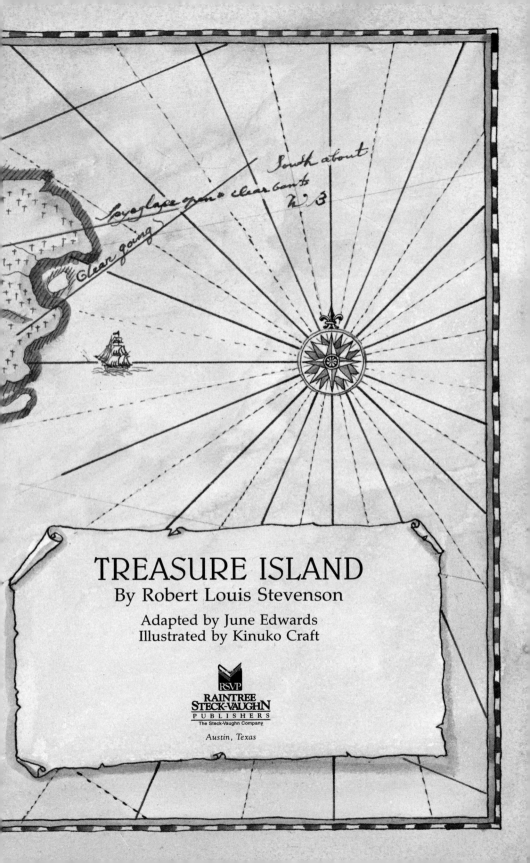

TREASURE ISLAND
By Robert Louis Stevenson

Adapted by June Edwards
Illustrated by Kinuko Craft

RSVP
**RAINTREE
STECK-VAUGHN**
P U B L I S H E R S
The Steck-Vaughn Company

Austin, Texas

Copyright © 1991 Steck-Vaughn Company

Copyright © 1980 Raintree Publishers Limited Partnership

Library of Congress Number: 79-24100

Library of Congress Cataloging-in-Publication Data

Edwards, June.
  Treasure Island.

  (Raintree short classics)
  SUMMARY: While going through the possessions of a deceased guest who owed them money, the mistress of the inn and her son find a treasure map that leads them to a pirate's fortune.
  [1. Buried treasure—Fiction. 2. Pirates—Fiction. 3. Adventure stories] I. Stevenson, Robert Louis, 1850–1894. Treasure Island. II Craft, Kinuko. III. Title.
PZ7.E2563Tr   [Fic.]   79-24100

ISBN 0-8172-1655-3 hardcover library binding

ISBN 0-8114-6844-5 softcover binding

27 28 04 03

CONTENTS

BILLY BONES

1

I remember the first time I saw the old seaman. He had come to the Admiral Benbow Inn, which my father owned, singing:

"Fifteen men on the dead man's chest—
Yo-ho-ho, and a bottle of rum!"

His hair was tied in a pigtail and a white scar lay across one cheek. Beside him was a large sea chest.

"Bring me a glass of rum!" he roared. He drank it slowly and looked about at the inn.

"This is where I'll stay," he said. "You can call me captain. All I'll want is rum and bacon and eggs." He threw four gold pieces on the counter to pay for room and board.

Each day the captain walked along the cliffs looking through a brass telescope. At night he sat in the parlor near the fire and drank rum. He spoke few words. We and the other guests left him alone. One time he took me aside.

"There's a silver fourpenny every month for you, Jim," he whispered, "if you'll keep your eye open for a one-legged sailor. Let me know the minute you see him."

Months went by while the captain stayed at the inn. He owed us more money, but we dared not ask for it. During this time my father became very ill. My mother and I ran the inn by ourselves. One morning, while the captain was out, a strange man came into the parlor. Two fingers were missing from his left hand.

"Come here, sonny," he said. "Is me mate Billy Bones in this house?"

"I don't know, sir," I answered.

"He has a scar on his right cheek."

"Oh, you mean the captain. He's out walking," I said.

I stepped outside to look down the road. The man ordered me back in with an oath that burned my ears. Then he smiled and patted me on the shoulder.

"Here comes me mate, Bill. Bless his ole heart. Let's just you and me surprise him, sonny. He'll like that."

He pushed me behind the door and pulled out his cutlass. I could hear him swallow hard. The captain marched in and started across the floor.

"Bill!" called the stranger loudly. The captain spun around on his heel. His face turned pale.

"Black Dog!" he gasped.

"Who else? Come to see me old shipmate, Bill."

"So, you've run me down. What do you want?"

"Well, now. Let's have a glass of rum and talk things over."

I ran to get the rum. When I returned, Black Dog ordered me to leave the room. For a long time I could hear only a murmur from the parlor. Then the voices grew louder.

"No, no, no!" cried the captain. "Swing one, swing all, say I."

The chairs and table crashed to the floor. I heard a clash of steel and a cry of pain. Black Dog ran out the inn door. Blood was streaming down the captain's shoulder.

"You're hurt!" I cried.

"Get me rum, Jim," he gasped. "I have to get away from here."

I was rushing to get it when I heard him fall. My mother ran downstairs. We raised the man's head. His skin was a deathly white.

"Oh, dear," cried my mother. "If only your father were not so sick."

Just then the door opened. In walked Dr. Livesey to see my father.

"This man has had a stroke," said the doctor. "Jim, get me a bowl."

The doctor ripped the captain's sleeve to the shoulder. While I held the bowl, he cut into a vein and let out blood. With great effort, we carried the seaman upstairs to bed.

"He should lie here a week," said Dr. Livesey. "Another stroke will kill him."

About noon I took the captain some medicine and a cold drink. He sat up and grabbed my arm.

"Jim, how long did the doctor say I should stay?" he asked.

"A week, at least," I replied.

"Thunder! A week! I can't do that. They'll have the black spot on me by then." He fell back onto his pillow and lay still.

"That sailor you saw today. Black Dog," he said after a while. "He's a bad one. But there's worse than him. If they tip me the black spot, ride your horse to the doctor. Tell him it's the sea chest they're after. Cap'n Flint gave it to me when he was dying."

"What's the black spot, captain?" I asked.

"I'll tell you if they give it to me." His voice grew weaker and he fell into a deep sleep.

That evening my poor father died. I had little time to think of the captain. The night before the funeral, the seaman came downstairs and helped himself at the bar. He shocked us by singing his ugly sea chanty:

"Fifteen men on the dead man's chest—
Yo-ho-ho, and a bottle of rum,
Drink and the devil had done for the rest—
Yo-ho-ho, and a bottle of rum!"

The next day, I was standing at the door of the inn. Down the road came a blind man, tapping the ground with a stick.

"Will any kind friend tell a poor old blind man where he may be?" he called.

"This is the Admiral Benbow Inn, sir," I answered.

"I hear a young voice. Give me your hand, lad, and lead me in."

The blind man gripped my hand tightly. He pulled me close and whispered.

9

"Now, boy, take me to the captain."

"Sir, I dare not."

"Take me," he hissed, "or I'll break your arm." He gave it a twist that made me cry out. I took him at once to the parlor. The captain's eyes filled with fear. The blind man pressed something into Bones' hand. Then he let go of my arm and left the inn. The black spot! The captain turned it over.

"Ten o'clock," he read. "That's only six hours!"

He sprang to his feet, then swayed and fell to the floor. The captain had died of another stroke.

THE SEA CHEST

2

There were no other guests in the inn. My mother and I ran down the road seeking help. A boy agreed to ride to town for us, and we went back to the inn alone.

"We must open the sea chest, Jim," my mother said. "He has owed us money for months. We'll take out only what is ours. We need it so badly now that your father is gone."

I found the key hanging around the captain's neck. We hurried upstairs to his bedroom. My mother turned the chest lock and threw back the lid. On top were clothes, tobacco, pistols, and a compass. Underneath were a bag of gold pieces and a bundle tied up in oilcloth.

The coins were from many countries. Counting our share took a long time. We were halfway through when I heard something on the road. The blind man's stick! We held our breaths. He rattled the bolt on the front door, but could not get in. We heard him tapping slowly away.

"Let's take what we've counted and go," cried my mother.

"I'll just take this to make it even," I said and grabbed the bundle. We ran downstairs and out into the dense fog. Soon we heard footsteps and saw a lantern.

"Take the money and run, Jim," said my mother. "I can't go on. I'm going to faint."

I helped her down the bank before she fell. Then I crept back up to see what was happening. Eight men came tearing down the road. In the middle was the blind man.

"Down with the door!" he ordered.

"Ay, ay, sir!" answered the men. They ran forward, then stood back, surprised to find the door already open.

"Go on!" shouted the blind man. "What's keeping you?" The men rushed inside the inn.

"Bill's dead," came a cry.

"Search him, you lubbers," yelled the blind man. "The rest of you, get the sea chest."

Several men ran upstairs. Soon a body leaned out of the window.

"Someone's already been here. They turned the chest inside out."

"Is it there?"

"The money is."

"It's not the money I want!" roared the blind man.

"We don't see it anywhere."

"It's those people in the inn. Find 'em!"

I could hear chairs being thrown and doors kicked in. Suddenly a whistle sounded.

"That's Dirk," cried a sailor. "We have to go, mates."

"They're close by, you fools!" shouted the blind man. "If only I had eyes. You'll be as rich as kings if you find 'em."

A tramp of horses sounded on the road. The seamen scattered, deserting the blind man, who stayed, tapping and calling for help. The horses topped the rise and galloped down the hill. The old man ran back and forth in confusion, and then ran right into the path of the horses. He screamed and fell dead under the animals' feet.

The riders pulled up, horrified. They had come from town to help us. My mother was better, so we all went back to the inn. The place was torn apart and the money gone from the sea chest.

"If they got the money, why did they tear the place apart?" asked a rider. "What else were they after?"

"It must have been this," I said. I took the bundle from my pocket. "I want to carry it right now to Dr. Livesey."

I climbed up behind a rider and rode hard to the doctor's house. He was visiting with another gentleman, Squire Trelawney.

"Bravo!" shouted the squire when he heard the story. "Captain Flint was one of the most bloodthirsty pirates that ever sailed. He'd do anything for money."

The doctor picked up the bundle I had brought.

"What would you do, Trelawney, if this were a clue to where Flint buried some treasure?"

"Why, I'd outfit a ship and take you and Jim Hawkins along. We'd find that treasure if it took a year."

"Well, Jim. Shall we open it?"

"Yes, sir!" I cried.

Inside we found a sealed paper and a book. In the book were lists of numbers covering twenty years. A date was on one side and a sum of money on the other. On the last page was a total and the words, "Bones, his pile."

"I can't make head or tail of this," said Dr. Livesey.

"It's as clear as noonday," cried the squire. "This is the blackhearted dog's account-book. The sums are the scoundrel's share in his pirate robberies. But what about the other paper?"

The doctor opened the seals on the paper. Out fell a map of an island. In the middle of the land was a hill called Spyglass. Three crosses were marked in red ink. On the back was more information:

"Tall tree, Spy-glass shoulder, bearing a point to the N. of N.N.E.

"Skeleton Island E.S.E. by E.

"Ten feet.

"The silver can be found by following the east hill, ten fathoms south of the black rock with the face on it.

"J. F."

"I'll have a ship ready in three weeks!" declared the squire. "Hawkins here will be the cabin boy and you, Livesey, will be the ship's doctor."

"I'll go," said the doctor. "But remember, we're not the only ones who know of this map. We must not breathe a word of this to anyone."

Trelawney went to Bristol to find a ship. Weeks passed before a letter came. The gentleman had bought a schooner called the *Hispaniola* and hired a cook named Long John Silver. With the seaman's help, a full crew was found.

I said good-bye to my mother and took a stage to meet the squire. The doctor, who had gone to London, also received a letter and headed for Bristol.

The day after I arrived, the squire sent me with a note to a tavern owned by John Silver. I remembered Billy Bones' warning when I saw the huge, one-legged man leaning on a crutch. But the cook was so friendly and cheerful, I was not afraid.

"Mr. Silver, sir?" I said, holding out the note.

"Yes, my lad. And who might you be?"

"Jim Hawkins, sir. Your new cabin boy."

A man sitting across the room rose and ran for the door. My heart leaped into my mouth.

"Stop him! It's Black Dog!" I yelled.

"Who?" asked Long John. "I don't believe I know the name."

"He's a bloodthirsty pirate," I cried. "Didn't the squire tell you?"

"What! In my house! Was that you drinking with him, Morgan?"

The man called Morgan came forward slowly.

"Now, Morgan," said Long John, very sternly, "you never saw that Black Dog before, did you?"

"Not I, sir," said Morgan.

"You didn't know his name, did you?"

"No, sir."

"By the powers, Morgan, it's just as well for you!" said Silver, and sent him back to his seat. "Well, I'm afraid your man got away, Jim. What a pity."

When I returned from the tavern, Dr. Livesey, Squire Trelawney and I went to see the *Hispaniola*. While we were in the cabin, the captain knocked on the door. I could see that he and the squire did not get along.

"Well, Captain Smollett, what do you want?" asked the ship's owner.

"I'm sorry to say this, sir. But I don't like this trip and I don't like the men."

"Why not?" asked Livesey.

"When I was hired I did not know we were going after treasure. I learned that from the sailors. I don't like treasure hunts. Bad things happen."

"Is that all?"

"I should have chosen my own crew, sir. The mate can't handle the men and the sailors all seem to know about a treasure map."

"I never told them!" cried the squire.

"Right now they're putting powder and arms in the forehold instead of under the cabin. I insist on changing them or I shall quit my job."

The squire agreed, but his dislike of Smollett grew stronger. Later, when the captain shouted at me to get to work, I felt the same way.

THE APPLE BARREL

3

We set sail for Treasure Island the next morning. The *Hispaniola* was a good ship and the captain knew his business. The friendliest sailor on board was the cook, Long John Silver. He kept a parrot in a cage in one corner of the galley.

"Come, Hawkins," the man would say. "Come talk to old John and Cap'n Flint. I calls my parrot Cap'n Flint after the famous pirate."

"Pieces of eight! Pieces of eight! Pieces of eight!" the parrot would scream until John threw a cloth over the cage.

On deck was a barrel of apples for the sailors to eat. One day, shortly before we reached the island, I decided I wanted one. Only a few were left, so I climbed all the way into the barrel. Sitting inside in the dark with the ship rocking, I fell asleep. Suddenly, someone sat down on the deck and leaned against the barrel. I started to rise when I heard the voice of Long John Silver. After a few words, I lay there trembling in fear.

"How long are we going to wait, Silver? I've had my fill of Cap'n Smollett," said the sailor called Israel Hands.

"You'll keep quiet till I give the word," answered Silver. "We'll wait till the squire and doctor find the treasure and get it aboard. When the time comes, we'll let her rip."

"Land ho!" shouted the lookout. Feet rushed across the deck. Slipping outside the barrel, I ran to join Dr. Livesey.

"I have terrible news, sir. Get the captain and squire to the cabin quick."

The three gentlemen went below. I told them everything I had heard from the apple barrel.

"I'm sorry, Captain Smollett," said the squire. "You were right about the men. Tell us what to do."

"Well, sir," said the captain. "We can't turn back now. Until the treasure is found, we have some time. Let's gather the servants and any sailors who are on our side and strike when the pirates least expect it."

I now hated the thought of Treasure Island. The air was hot and muggy. The sailors lay about on deck and refused to work. It was Long John Silver who pushed them to their duties.

"Sir," said the captain to the squire. "The men are in a dreadful mood. I think we should let them go ashore for the afternoon. Silver will keep them in line. He wants order as much as we do."

A cheer went up when the captain gave the leave. The seamen rushed to the boats. On an impulse, I slipped over the side and curled up in the fore-sheets of the nearest vessel. As it neared the island, I caught a tree branch and swung out to the beach. I ran as fast as I could through the bushes till I could run no more.

Before long I heard Silver's voice. He was talking to Tom, one of the squire's sailors.

"I'd rather die like a dog, Silver," Tom said, "then join your mess of swabs."

The brave man turned his back and started toward the beach. With a cry, Long John grabbed a branch and hurled it through the air. It hit Tom hard in the back. His hands flew up as he gasped and fell. Silver leaped on top of the sailor and drove a knife into his back. The world spun before my eyes. When I came to, John was wiping his knife on the grass. I slipped quietly away and ran from the killer.

As I rushed down the hill, a stone rolled in front of me. I saw something dark and shaggy leap behind a tree. For a moment I could not move. I started back up the hill and the creature circled round in front. I gripped my pistol and walked boldly forward. To my surprise, a man dropped on his knees before me.

"Who are you?" I gasped.

"Ben Gunn," he answered in a rusty voice. "I haven't spoken to anyone for three long years."

"Were you shipwrecked?"

"Nay, mate. Marooned."

I had heard the word. When pirates did not like a mate, they put him off on an empty island with only a little gunpowder.

"Three years I've lived on goats and berries," moaned Ben Gunn. "Cheese is what I've dreamed of. Would you have some?"

"If I can get on board ship again," I said, "you can have all you want."

"Jim," he whispered after I told him my name. "I'm rich. You'll be glad you found me."

I was sure the man had gone crazy all alone on the island. A shadow came over his face. He grasped my arm.

"Ain't that Flint's ship?" he asked and pointed to the *Hispaniola*.

"No, Flint is dead, but some of his hands are on board."

"Not a man with one leg!" he cried.

"Long John Silver? He's the cook and the pirate ringleader." Then I told him the fix my friends and I were in.

"You're a good lad, Jim," said the maroon and patted me on the head. "Just put your trust in old Ben."

Gunn had been on Flint's ship when the treasure was buried. Billy Bones was the mate and John Silver the quartermaster. Flint and six strong men had gone ashore, but only Flint came back. The others were killed. No one knew how. Three years ago Gunn was on another ship when he spotted the island. He told his mates of the treasure. For twelve days the sailors searched, but could not find it. When the ship sailed again, the angry men left him marooned on the island.

A cannon thundered from the ship.

"They've begun to fight!" I cried. The sound of smaller guns filled the air. Soon we saw in front of us a British flag flying above the woods.

"That's the fort made years ago by Cap'n Flint," said Ben Gunn.

"Let's go, Ben," I said. "My friends must be in there."

"You go," he said. "I'll be where I was today. If anyone comes for me, he must wave a white cloth."

A cannonball tore through the trees. Ben and I flew off in different directions. I ran from place to place with balls crashing around me. When I neared the house, I called to those inside. They were very glad to see me.

I learned that Squire Trelawney and his servants, Dr. Livesey, Captain Smollett, and one of the sailors had left the ship in a boat. They rowed to a wooden stockade they could see on the island. The shots came from Silver's crew on ship and those on land. One of the servants and several pirates were killed. I, in turn, told them of my meeting with Ben Gunn.

Late that night we heard the pirates roaring and singing on the beach. They were drunk with rum. I lay down and slept like a log until morning.

THE ATTACK

4

"Flag of truce!" I heard someone shout. "Why it's Silver himself."

I jumped up, rubbing my eyes, and ran to see. Two men were standing outside the wall waving a white cloth.

"Keep indoors, mates," the captain said. "It's likely a trick." Then he called to the pirates.

"Who goes? What do you want?"

"Silver," called the other man. "He wants to come up and talk."

We watched the one-legged cook struggle up the hill. His crutch kept slipping in the soft sand.

"Good morning to you all," he called cheerily.

"Whatever you have to say, say it," snapped Captain Smollett.

"All right, I'll get to the point," answered Silver. "We want that treasure and we'll have it. You have a chart, don't you?"

"Maybe," said Smollett.

"You give us the map and we'll give you a fair share of the treasure. When we leave, I'll tell the first ship I see to come get you."

"Is that all?"

"If you refuse," growled Silver, "all you'll get from me is cannonballs."

"You'll never find that treasure, Silver," barked Smollett. "And your good-for-nothing men will never be able to sail that ship. If I ever see you again I'll put a bullet in you."

Silver spat on the ground. With a dreadful oath he stumbled off, sliding down the sandy hill into the woods.

"Men," said the captain. "They'll be back. We're outnumbered, but we're inside a fort. I think we can take them."

An hour passed as we made ready to fight. Muskets were loaded and cutlasses laid out. Each man watched several windows while I stood by to help load.

"I see one!" shouted a servant and fired his musket.

Bullets struck the stockade, but none came in.

"Did you hit him?" asked the captain when all was quiet.

"I don't think so, sir."

Before long a shout rang out. Several buccaneers leaped from behind trees and ran straight toward the house. Others opened fire from the woods. A ball came through the doorway and smashed the doctor's musket.

Silver's men climbed over the fence like monkeys. We hit three, but four kept coming. They were soon upon us, shooting their muskets and flashing their swords.

"Out, lads! Fight 'em in the open!" shouted the captain.

I grabbed a cutlass and dashed out the door. Around the corner came a buccaneer. He swung his sword at me. I leaped aside, slipped in the sand, and rolled down the hill. When I was on my feet again, the victory was ours. Seven of Silver's men were killed and three had run away.

"Back to the house!" cried Captain Smollett. I ran full speed up the hill. We had won the battle, but paid a price. Two of the servants were dead and the captain badly wounded.

"At least," said Smollett weakly, "the odds are better now. We were seven men to nineteen when we left the ship. Now it's four to nine."

We saw no more of the buccaneers the rest of the day. After lunch, the squire and doctor went to a corner to talk. Soon the doctor took up his pistols and cutlass. He slung a musket over his shoulder and set off through the trees.

"If I'm right, he's going to see Ben Gunn," I thought.

The day grew very hot. I longed to be out in the cool woods. In the afternoon, I sneaked bread into my pockets, grabbed some bullets and pistols, and slipped out of the stockade. Ben Gunn had told me of a boat he had made and hidden, and I planned to find it.

Night came before I reached the white rock the maroon had described. Below, hidden in a hollow, was a tent of goatskins. Underneath was the boat. It was poorly made and very small, even for me.

Finding the boat made me so happy, I had another idea. I would cut the *Hispaniola* loose from her anchor! I ate my bread and watched the fog close in. The island was pitch black. Only the pirates' fire on shore and the ship's light could be seen.

Ben's boat was very hard to row. Round and round I went in circles. Had it not been for the tide, I would never have reached the ship at all. When I was finally alongside her, I took my knife and cut each rope strand until only two were left. I lay waiting for the rope to loosen.

Loud voices came from inside the cabin. I listened carefully. Two drunken seamen were yelling at each other. I knew the voice of Israel Hands. At last a breeze came and the ship moved. With effort I cut the last two strands. I was almost slammed against the ship. A cord hung down. I grabbed it and pulled myself up until I could see inside the cabin. Each sailor had a hand on the other's throat.

I dropped back into the little boat, and none too soon. It jerked suddenly and changed course. I froze with fear. The tide was taking me out to sea! I lay in the boat's bottom and waited for death. For hours it rose and fell with the waves. At last I slept, dreaming of home and the Admiral Benbow Inn.

The sun was shining brightly when I awoke. The boat tossed around at the southwest end of Treasure Island. I wanted to row ashore, but was afraid of being dashed against the rocks. I lay again on the bottom and let the boat go its own way.

The sun was high and very hot. Seawater dried my skin and caked my lips with salt. I longed for a drink of water. The current carried me round the point of the island. In front of me, a half-mile away, was the *Hispaniola* under sail.

I was surprised to see the ship moving to and fro with the wind. No one was steering. The men must be either drunk or dead, I thought. More than anything I wanted to go on board and return the vessel to Captain Smollett. With all my strength I rowed toward the ship. I was on top of a wave when suddenly the *Hispaniola* turned. Its bow swung over my head. I leaped from my boat and caught the boom. While I hung there, the ship went down and smashed my little boat. I was left on board with no way back to the island.

CAPTAIN JIM HAWKINS

5

I had almost gained my footing when the jib flapped and filled. The ship heeled over and I tumbled onto the deck. Nearby lay the two sailors I had seen earlier. One was dead and the other, Israel Hands, was wounded.

"Brandy," murmured Hands.

I ran downstairs into the cabin. The floor was thick with blood and mud. Empty bottles clinked together. I found brandy for Hands and food for me. I took a huge drink from a keg of water and returned to deck.

"Where did you come from?" growled Hands.

"I've come to take over the ship," I declared. "You can call me captain now."

He looked at me glumly.

"I don't like that flag," I declared. "I'm taking it down. Better none than this one." I pulled down the black pirate flag and threw it overboard.

Israel watched me closely. Finally he muttered, "I suppose, Cap'n Hawkins, you'll want to get to shore soon."

"Why, yes, with all my heart."

"Well, then, you're going to need my help. That man's dead and you don't know nothing about sailing. Give me food and drink and tie up my leg and I'll tell you what to do."

"That's fair and square," I said. "But I'm not going back to the same place to anchor. I'm going to beach at North Inlet."

Hands agreed and I soon had the ship sailing along

grandly. I was very proud of being ship's captain. The weather was bright and pleasant. I had plenty of food and water. The only thing that worried me was the pirate, Israel Hands.

"Step down in the cabin, like a good lad, and fetch me some wine. This brandy's too strong for my head," he said after a while.

I looked at him in surprise. No sailor ever wanted wine over brandy. I did not like the way he was smiling.

"Do you want white or red wine?" I asked, trying to hide my fears.

"Don't matter."

"I'll bring you some port if I can find any," I said and raced noisily down the deck. I slipped off my shoes and crept back along the other side to watch the pirate. He was on his hands and knees, dragging his leg across the floor. He reached a coil of rope and a knife, then quickly crawled back to his old place. That was what I wanted to know. Israel could move about and he was now armed. He would soon try to kill me, but not before the ship was beached. I stole back to the cabin, put on my shoes, and grabbed a bottle of wine. When I reached the deck, Hands was lying as I had left him. He pulled out a stick of tobacco.

"Cut me a chunk of that, Jim," he said weakly. "I ain't got no knife and no strength to use one. I'm not long for this world."

"Then you'd better say your prayers," I snapped.

Getting the *Hispaniola* into North Inlet was not easy, but Hands was a good pilot. I was so busy with the ship that I forgot the danger I was in. A sudden quiet made me turn my head. Israel was halfway toward me with a knife in his hand. He charged like a roaring bull! I screamed and let go of the tiller. It swung and struck him in the chest. I drew my pistol and fired, but nothing happened. The powder was wet with seawater.

The sailor was on his feet again and coming fast across the deck. Suddenly the ship struck ground and leaned

over. Both of us fell and rolled down the deck. I leaped for the sails and climbed hand over hand until I reached the cross-trees. The pirate looked up with hate in his eyes. I recharged my pistols as Israel started up the masts with the knife in his teeth.

"One more step, Mr. Hands," I called, "and I'll blow your brains out."

He stopped and took his knife from his mouth. Something sang through the air like an arrow. I felt a blow and a sharp pang. I was pinned by the shoulder to the mast! Both my pistols went off and dropped from my grasp. I heard a loud cry and saw Israel Hands fall into the waters below.

The knife had gone through my jacket but only pierced my skin. The wound was not deep. With a shudder I jerked free of the mast. Slowly, I climbed down to the deck.

The inlet water was shallow, so I dropped overboard and waded ashore. I headed toward the stockade. It was dark when I neared the house. I could hear my friends snoring inside. I tiptoed in, planning to lie down in my old place. Suddenly a shrill voice screamed out, "Pieces of eight! Pieces of eight!" It was Silver's parrot, Cap'n Flint. The sleepers awoke and sprang up.

"Who goes?" cried Silver. I turned to run, but a pirate grabbed me.

"So," said the cook. "Here's Jim Hawkins. Dropped in to see us, did you? What a nice surprise."

"Why are you here?" I demanded.

Silver told me that Dr. Livesey had come yesterday and offered them the house and the treasure map. My friends had gone, but he did not know where.

"What am I to do, then?" I asked.

"If you like the service, well, you'll join us," said Silver, "and if you don't, Jim, why, you're free to answer no."

I could feel the threat of death that overhung me. My heart beat painfully in my chest.

"Well, let the worst come to worst, it's little I care," I said. "I've seen too many die since I fell in with you. But

there's a thing or two I have to tell you," I continued, growing bolder, "and the first is this: your whole business has gone to wreck, and if you want to know who did it — it was I! I was in the apple barrel the night we sighted land, and heard you talking, and told every word before the hour was out. And as for your schooner, I have cut her cable, and killed the man you had aboard of her. I've taken her where you'll never see her again. Kill me, if you please, but the laugh's on my side!"

I stopped, out of breath. The men sat staring at me like sheep. All at once a pirate yelled and sprang for me with his knife.

"Avast there!" shouted Silver. "I'm the cap'n here. Leave the boy alone. I like him. He's more a man than the whole lot of you."

My heart beat hard against my chest. Silver leaned on the wall and lit a pipe. The pirates looked at him sullenly, then drew back and whispered together.

"You seem to have a lot to say," said Silver. "Pipe up and let me hear it."

"Well, sir," replied one of the pirates, "you're pretty free with the rules. This crew's dissatisfied; this crew don't like being bullied. We claim our right to a council." And one by one they stepped out the door. The cook and I were left alone in the house.

"Look here, Jim Hawkins," whispered Long John Silver. "They're going to throw me over and kill you. You're a good lad. I'll stand by you."

"You mean all's lost?" I cried.

"Ay, I do," he answered. "I'll save your life if I can. If we both come out alive, maybe you can save this old sea dog from hanging."

I looked out the window.

"Here they come!" I cried.

The door opened and the five men stepped inside. One came forward slowly and passed something to Silver.

"The black spot. I thought so," said Silver. He pulled the

treasure map from his pocket and threw it on the floor. The pirates leaped upon it like a cat on a mouse.

"Find yourself another cap'n. I'm done with it," he said.

But the men had changed their minds. Now that they had the map, they wanted Silver still to be their chief.

"Well, then," sneered the one-legged sailor. "This black spot ain't much good after all." He tossed the circle to me.

The men had another round of brandy, then lay down to sleep. Silver snored peacefully. But I lay awake half the night with dreadful thoughts.

THE SEARCH

6

"Ahoy!" shouted a voice in the morning. "Here's the doctor."

"Top o' the morning to you, sir," called Silver brightly. "We found a surprise for you."

"Not Jim!" exclaimed the doctor.

"The very same."

Dr. Livesey came into the house. He nodded at me, then went to the pirates to tend their wounds.

"I'd like to talk to that boy, please," he said when he was through.

"No!" shouted a buccaneer.

"Silence!" roared Silver. "Jim, will you give your word not to run away?"

"Cross my heart," I said.

"Well, doctor. Go down the hill a ways and I'll bring the boy to you."

There was a loud outcry inside the house. Silver called the men fools and waved the chart in their faces. He stomped out on his crutch toward the doctor.

"This lad will tell you how I saved his life," croaked Silver to Dr. Livesey. He then moved back to a tree stump and began to whistle.

"Jim, I can't leave you here," whispered Dr. Livesey. "Jump over the fence and run for it."

"No, I gave my word," I answered. "But I want you to know about the ship. It's in North Inlet."

"The ship!" exclaimed the doctor. I quickly told him all that had happened.

"It's always you, Jim, who saves our lives. We won't let you lose yours."

The doctor called to Long John.

"Silver! Don't be in a hurry to hunt for that treasure."

"What do you mean?" asked the cook, coming closer.

"I can't tell you any more. Keep the boy close to you. Good-bye, Jim."

The doctor shook my hand, nodded to Silver, and rushed off into the woods.

"Jim," said Silver when we were alone, "if I saved your life, you saved mine. I seen the doctor telling you to run, and I seen you say no. This is the first hope I had since the attack failed, and I owe it to you. You and me must stick close now, back to back like, and we'll save our necks in spite o' fate."

The men had made a huge fire, and they were cooking three times as much food as they needed as we walked back.

"Well, mates," said Silver when we returned. "They've got the ship, but I don't know where. Let's find the treasure, then hunt for the *Hispaniola*. I'll take care of Jim, here. He might come in handy."

My spirits sank. Long John Silver, who had double-crossed his men, would surely do the same for me. We set out with the chart to find the buried gold. Each pirate was armed to the teeth. On the cook's shoulder sat the parrot, Cap'n Flint. Silver tied a rope around my waist and led me like a dancing bear.

We followed the directions on the map. The way grew steep and rocky. Silver and I followed behind the rest. At times I had to give him a hand, or he would have fallen backwards down the slope.

A shout came from atop the hill. When we reached the place, a chill struck my heart. At the foot of a big pine lay a skeleton. His feet pointed in one direction. His hands, raised over his head like a diver's, pointed in the other.

"It's one of Flint's jokes, by thunder," said Silver. "It's

39

one of the men he killed. Look, he's laid him out like a compass. E.S.E. by E., just like on the chart."

We started up again, but this time the pirates kept close together and hardly spoke. The bones had scared them. When we stopped to rest, we could see many miles on all sides. Before us was Cape of the Woods. Behind was Skeleton Island and the open sea. Above rose Spyglass Hill. The only sound was that of the waves hitting the rocks below.

Suddenly from the woods in front came a thin, high voice singing:

"Fifteen men on the dead man's chest—
Yo-ho-ho, and a bottle of rum."

The men's faces went ghostly white. Some leaped to their feet. Others fell moaning to the ground.

"It's Flint's spirit," cried a sailor.

"Come, now," said Silver, his voice trembling. "It must be someone playing a trick."

"Darby M'Graw," wailed the voice. "Darby M'Graw. Fetch aft the rum, Darby!"

The buccaneers froze. Their eyes bugged out.

"Them was Flint's last words," gasped a pirate. Silver's teeth rattled in his head, but he spoke bravely.

"I wasn't afraid of Flint alive. I'll face him dead. I'm going after that treasure."

Silver rose to go, but the men did not move.

"That voice had an echo to it," added Silver. "Whoever heard of a ghost with an echo?"

"Well, that's so," said one of the men. "Besides it didn't really sound like Flint. It sounded more like. . .like . . ."

"Like Ben Gunn!" roared Silver.

"But he's dead, too."

"Yes, but who cares?" snorted a seaman. "Nobody minds Ben Gunn."

The color came back into the men's faces. They chatted together, then picked up their tools and started on. At last we neared the top of Spyglass Hill. Rising two hundred feet above us was a giant tree. Beneath, said the map, lay seven hundred thousand pounds in gold. Long John jerked at the rope that held me. He cursed the flies and swore at the men. He hoped, I am sure, to dig up the coins, find the ship, kill every person on the island, and sail away alone.

The pirates raced ahead. Their eyes burned with the thought of riches. Suddenly they stopped and gave a low cry. Before them was a large hole, with some grass growing in it, and a broken pick. The treasure had already been found. The gold was gone!

HOME AT LAST

7

The buccaneers, screaming oaths, leaped into the hole and dug with their fingers. Then they turned on their chief.

"You lubber! You knew all along it was gone. Look at his face!" Silver did not move. He looked as cool as ever.

"Let's after 'em, mates! It's only an old cripple and a boy."

A pirate was raising his arm to shoot when three bullets flashed from the trees. Two men fell headfirst into the pit. The other three turned and ran with all their might. Dr. Livesey and Ben Gunn came forward to join us.

"So, it *was* you, Ben Gunn," said Long John.

As we walked back down the hill, the doctor told us what happened. Three months ago Ben had found the treasure. He dug it up and carried it, in many trips, to a large cave. When the doctor learned of this, he went to Silver and gave him the useless chart and the house. My friends moved into the cave with Ben. After finding me at the stockade, the doctor got help and headed toward Spyglass Hill. Ben Gunn ran on ahead to scare the pirates.

"Ah," said Silver. "It's a good thing I had Jim here. Otherwise you would have cut me down, too. Eh, doctor?"

"Ay, ay," said Dr. Livesey cheerily.

When we reached the cave, Captain Smollett was lying before a big fire, still recovering from his wounds. Great heaps of coins and gold bars were in the corner. We ate a large meal of salted goat and wine. Never had anything tasted so good. Long John became the friendly seaman I had first met. But this time none of us were taken in.

The next morning we began the work of moving the treasure. It was one mile by land to the beach and three miles by boat to the *Hispaniola*. Day after day the work went on. One night we heard the drunken runaway buccaneers singing on the beach. We did not dare take them with us on the ship, but we left gunpowder, food, tools, and medicine.

At last we were ready to sail. As we drifted out of North Inlet, we saw the men on shore begging us not to leave them. Ben Gunn laughed with glee. I felt sorry for them, but knew they would only be hung for piracy if we took them home.

We headed for the nearest port in Spanish America and reached it at sundown. Squire Trelawney, Dr. Livesey and I went to hunt for a new crew. When we returned hours later, Long John Silver was gone. He had slipped away and taken a large bag of coins. We were happy to be rid of him so cheaply.

With our new seamen, we had a good trip home. The treasure was split among those of us who had first sailed on the *Hispaniola* and Ben Gunn. Of the one-legged pirate we heard no more.

I returned from Treasure Island richer and wiser. But nothing could ever drag me back. Sometimes at night I hear the waves booming against the coast. I start upright in bed. The voice of Cap'n Flint rings again in my ears:

"Pieces of eight! Pieces of eight! Pieces of eight!"

GLOSSARY

buccaneer *see* pirate

chanty (shant′ ē) a song that is sung by sailors as they work

compass (kəm′ pəs) an instrument that shows directions with a needle that always points to the north

cutlass (kət′ ləs) a short curved sword

musket (məs′ kət) a gun with a long barrel, used at one time by infantry soldiers

pirate (pī′ rət) someone who robs ships at sea; also called buccaneer

quartermaster (kwôrt′ ər mas′ tər) a ship's officer who takes care of the ship's steering and signals

schooner (skoo′ nər) a large ship with two masts

skeleton (skel′ ət ən) the framework of bones inside a person

squire (skwīr) a man in England who owns a lot of land

stockade (stäk ād′) a place closed off by a strong fence made of upright posts